ISBN 978-1-0980-3485-6 (paperback)
ISBN 978-1-0980-3486-3 (digital)

Christian Faith Publishing, Inc.
832 Park Avenue
Meadville, PA 16335
www.christianfaithpublishing.com

Cover Design and Interior Illustrations by: Nejla Shojaie
Cover Graphics and Interior Graphics by: Ngarlege Ngarndingabe

Printed in the United States of America

God spoke to Adam from heaven above.
Said, "Name all my creatures I made with love!"
So Adam went to work immediately.
He named every animal from A to Z.

1

This funny lookin' mammal has a long snout.
It digs in the dirt to root the bugs out.
It eats lots of termites—but the ants taste sweeter.
That's its favorite food so will call it ANTEATER!

Oh my gosh! Look what I see!
Eatin' fruit on the banana tree.
I bet'cha he'll eat a bunch of grapes.
Don't think so! Guess I will call it the APE!

3

I just saw a creature lyin' under some trees,
Not a care in the world restin' on grass and leaves.
Look at it nappin' and it's not even noon.
What shall I call it? I know! It's a BABOON!

This bad critter looked so mean.
It bucked and bucked and kicked and screamed.
It wears a long goatee under its chin.
BILLYGOAT I named him—I just can't win!

"Naah,
Naah"

Eating honey from the tree,
With big black fur did Adam see.
Hey you! Come on down from there!
I'm gonna' call you the big BLACK BEAR!

6

This one is crouchin' on a branch up high.
It's stalkin' its prey with hungry dark eyes.
It might climb down for food with a bribe.
I'll name it BOBCAT because of its size.

"Grrrr"

Hey! Big fella I'm callin' time out!
It's in the no-zone just look at its snout.
It's huffin' and puffin' and snortin', he is mad!
Gonna' name this the red BULL—watch out he is bad!

This perky fella has pink ears and cottontail.
It can outsmart the turtle and outrun the snail.
It will eat all the carrots in your veggie patch.
Why, this BUNNY leaves pellets all over the grass!

It has three stomachs to store its food.
With his teeth he laughs as he chews and chews.
This funny mammal has a huge bump;
CAMEL—the only name that fits this lump!

"Meow"

"Here kitty! Here kitty!" Now where is he at?
I keep callin' his name. Ah! He's takin' a nap.
He slobbers on my lap as he licks his paw,
That's Harry my CAT—he meows when I call!

11

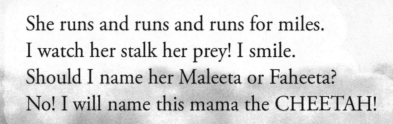

She runs and runs and runs for miles.
I watch her stalk her prey! I smile.
Should I name her Maleeta or Faheeta?
No! I will name this mama the CHEETAH!

Out on a limb it was swingin',
His hands wrapped around it clingin'.
Hey! You high up in the tree!
You I'll name the CHIMPANZEE!

"Hoo,
Hoo, Hoo"

13

It sneaks so quietly tracking its prey.
If I were its lunch I'd begin to pray,
"God spare my life I'd plead today!
It's a COUGAR Lord, please send it away!"

14

Out in the field chewin' its cud,
The grass was green, not one speck of mud.
On its belly four teats hung from the udder,
With big floppy ears, "It's a COW!" Adam muttered.

"MOO"

15

This mini antler will never grow tall,
Not like the Elk it will always be small.
He has tiny wee horns you can barely see.
In Africa's bush land this DIK-DIK runs free!

16

He's my one-eyed Jack 'cause he lost an eye,
Fightin' with a bulldog that was twice his size.
He's gettin' pretty old and diapers he must wear.
He's Gismo my DOG and he pees *eveerrryyy* where.

"HEE-HAW"

It's buckin' and kickin' and won't leave its stall,
Won't carry its load and won't heed my call.
It's up to *noooooo* good showin' its teeth with a smirk.
I'll call it DONKEY—this mockin' jackass is a jerk!

18

She laughs and sprays water to cool off her rump,
Sports thick ivory husks on each side of her trunk.
She has big floppy ears and her color is gray.
I'll call this an ELEPHANT—she loves to play!

19

On again…off again…look at that sight!
In summer it's brown—in winter it's white!
Its soft thick fur is like precious gold.
This ERMINE keeps you warm when it's cold.

His tall neck stretches up to the sky,
He eats leaves off trees he reaches up high.
His legs are too long to give him a bath.
He is so comical I'll call him GIRAFFE!

22

"Good golly!" said Adam, "Look what I found!
Pokin' its head up from the ground!
It'll hide its face if you come around.
I'll name it GROUNDHOG—it lives underground!"

This friendly rodent loves to eat and play,
Runnin' many laps all around its cage.
It isn't scary like its auntie the rat.
Keep this tiny HAMSTER from Brewster the cat.

This ugly creature has a pig-like snout.
Spines cover its fur to keep predators out.
It dines on insects and as a pretense,
This HEDGEHOG curls in a ball for a defense.

"Grff,
Grff"

Looks like a cross 'tween a pig and baby whale.
To mark his space flings its poop with his tail.
His diet is plants he eats lots of grass.
The HIPPO meets humans—what a rowdy clash!

"Roowwarr"

"CACKLE CACKLE, AHH, HA, HA"

I hear the ghoulish laughter of Lol!
Sounds like it's comin' from the belly of hell.
You can hear the fiend howl on a moonlit night.
This HYENA makes animals tremble with fright!

It scampers through the hills, roams the land.
Its long curvy horns will buck you, so scram!
I think it came over on Noah's boat.
Will call it the IBEX—it's a wild goat!

She runs like the wind to catch her prey.
Can't outrun this feline, just ain't no way!
With spotty black spots and fur of golden brown,
A real cool JAGUAR—won't see her in town!

29

Here's another hopper short legs and all,
She'll box with her fists she ain't too tall.
She wears a big pouch to hop around the zoo,
To cart her babe I'll name her the KANGAROO!

30

So cute and cuddly all the kids will
       agree,
With big black eyes and huggin' the
       tree.
Starin' down at me with a black
       button nose,
KOALA—a sure fit from its head to
       its toes!

31

RRaaaaaaHHHHH

This hungry lookin' dude is covered with spots.
Take a closer look I think they're polka dots.
Do you want a toy you can ride and pet?
You can't ride this LEOPARD—that's a sure bet!

Throughout the forest you could hear,
A loud, loud roar—it caused great fear!
Adam watched her stand tall like a Queen.
I'll call your mate the proud LION KING!

This funny creature is smirkin' at me,
Eatin' the leaves off the branch on the tree.
This feisty female she's a big mama.
So let me call her the laughin' LLAMA!

34

With small squinty eyes, don't know how it can see.
Why, it's a little rodent lookin' up at me.
With a narrow snout it burrows deep in the hole.
It has real silky fur so will name it the MOLE.

"Eek,
Eek,
Eek"

This gutsy creature is mimickin' me,
Tossin' down apples from the top of the tree.
Makin' funny faces He chatters at me.
This spunky beast I will call the MONKEY.

36

"OOU-WAH"
"OOOOOH"

This creature has antlers six feet wide.
It bellows so loud to catch a mate to its side.
Has a long square face and loves to run loose,
With big floppy ears he looks just like a MOOSE.

Hee-haw-haw! Hee-haw! It said with a squawk,
As Adam tugged and tugged to make it walk.
When Adam sat down it kicked at the stool.
Adam yelled out, "Why, you're a stubborn MULE!"

"Hee-Haw"

38

It loves to hang out near Eucalyptus trees.
He's an Aussie—an endangered species, you see!
It hunts for termites' roots them out with its tongue.
This colorful NUMBAT will eat insects as crumbs.

This silly creature is drivin' me crazy.
I really can't believe that it's so lazy.
It's just too lazy to get up and eat.
Call it OPOSSUM—it's pretendin' to sleep!

40

These super-duper brutes will carry your load.
They will plow your field in the heat or cold.
They till the ground and they tread the hay.
These OXEN will work for hours all day.

41

Next I saw a curly tail so pink
Wallow in the mud as I watched it sink.
It squeaked and squealed tossin' mud about.
So I named it PIG because of its snout.

"Oi!"
"Oi!"

Its size is quite large it lives in the snow.
It catches fish with its claws. What a way to go!
It's mighty and strong doesn't have a care,
Can't cuddle in bed 'cause it's a POLAR BEAR.

Now, this frisky fella has a body with quills.
If you sneak up behind it you won't be thrilled.
Its needles will poke you from its behind.
Let's call this strange critter a PORCUPINE.

44

It's as cute as a button, but wild at heart,
Friend of humans steals their food when it's dark.
Adorable, curious, posing for a *selfie*;
This happy thief is QUOKKA—its newborn is a joey!

It marks its home with its own special scent,
Hisses and shrieks don't make a lick-a-sense.
Battles opponents it's a real wrestlin' match.
Foxes love this QUOLL—it's a yum-yum catch!

Adam hiked up and down the trail,
Saw four black eyes and two ringtails.
They scurried to hide till night's full moon.
Got the perfect name! Will call them RACCOON!

Caught in the thickets it's stuck in a noose.
Can't move its body, can't shake it loose.
All of its hooves are caught among thorns.
Call it a RAM—it has two horny horns!

Up in the attic late into the night,
Strange noises and clatter hidden from sight.
Sounds like a party goin' on unaware.
Hmm… I smell a RAT way yonder upstairs.

I'll sneak up behind it! Gotta' be quiet!
If I make a noise it could start a riot.
It sprouts a large horn just above its nose,
RHINOCEROS—call it from head to toes!

"Baa,Baa"

This one follows me wherever I go,
Its wooly coat is the color of snow.
It says, *Baa! Baa!* All it does is bleat.
Think this one's easy! I'll call it SHEEP!

51

This despicable critter has fur so black,
With double white stripes runnin' down its back.
It set off an odor—oh my, it stunk!
I got too close! Let me call it a SKUNK!

It scurries to the ground from a limb on the tree.
Cracks its nuts with his jaw starin' boldly at me.
The kids will love it. So let's give it a whirl!
I think I shall name it the little SQUIRREL.

53

Oh, my gosh! Take a look at this!
It trots, it jumps, it's doin' some tricks.
This royal beauty bows and neighs as it sings.
I call this white STALLION—truly fit for a king!

"Neigh,
Neigh"

Has stripes on its head and across its back.
Look at that! It's a big overstuffed cat.
With really sharp claws and a savage growl,
Can't tame this TIGER 'cause its nature is wild!

"GRRRROW"

This fella I created as I lay on my bed.
He was quite the comic as I drew it in my head.
He retrieved the cracked toy that I threw away.
Hey! Your name is UNIQUE 'cause you love to play.

This cunning shrew you don't want to rouse.
He waits to creep into the old hen house.
Set traps in the garden, it won't eat your crops.
Let's name it the VIXEN—it's a sly, sly fox!

57

This wild beast guards its land without fear.
Two massive husks sit between its ears.
To avoid his foes to the river he fled,
This WATERBUCK cools off in the riverbed.

58

This big white mammal lives where it's cold.
He stalks innocent prey huddled close in the fold.
Its favorite meal is the little white lamb.
I'll name it WHITE WOLF—its disguise is a sham!

Hey! What is that racket underneath the bush?
Snortin' and gruntin'—somethin' heavy it pushed.
Looks mean and ugly right down to its core.
It isn't a pet it's a WILD BOAR!

"WHUFF,
WHUFF"

He's not a happy camper livin' alone.
Dwells with a groupie! That's where he calls home.
His diet is insects, fruits, seeds and grains.
This fur ball is XERUS—will hide when it rains!

He is wild at birth until skillfully trained.
Runs through green meadows as it's lovingly tamed.
Children all love him! They're happy and glad!
I'll call this a YEARLING—it's just a young lad!

This one runs with painted stripes,
Across its back it's black and white.
Adam scratched his head and said, "Aha!
I got it. I'll call his name the ZEBRA!"

Then God looked down from heaven above,
Surveyed the creatures Adam named with love.
God smiled real big! He was *soooooo* pleased!
Exclaimed, "It's ALL GOOD!" "Yes," Adam agreed.

About the Author

Janet DeAngelo was born in Toledo, Ohio and comes from a military family. She followed her six siblings into the Armed Forces and served part of her tour in Europe. After her Honorable Discharge, she traveled across the country working in sales. Once Janet met and married her husband, they opened a prosperous wig business in the Jersey Shore and South Florida. After selling their business, she pursued a twenty-three year career as a renowned makeup artist for several reputable cosmetic companies. After her retirement, Janet shifted her focus to her other passion—writing. She wrote and published her first two books, then continued to become a staff writer for her church's newsletter. Although Janet writes in many literary genres, her favorite is humor by far! Reflecting on the name "Witty Wits", her statement is simple: "the world needs laughter". Janet currently resides in South Florida and since then has become an ordained minister. Now her purpose is to see children grow in the Lord and to minister in prayer. She has two children, four grandchildren and many wonderful friends.

CPSIA information can be obtained
at www.ICGtesting.com
Printed in the USA
BVHW020212200821
614843BV00018B/726

9 781098 034856